* The Next Door Series *

CONRAD
AND THE
Cowgirl
NEXT
DOOR

WRITTEN BY
Denette Fretz

ILLUSTRATED BY
Gene Barretta

ZONDERkidz

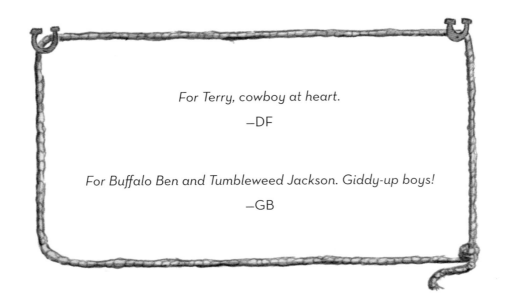

For Terry, cowboy at heart.

—DF

For Buffalo Ben and Tumbleweed Jackson. Giddy-up boys!

—GB

ZONDERKIDZ

Conrad and the Cowgirl Next Door
Copyright © 2014 by Denette Fretz
Illustrations © 2014 by Gene Barretta

Requests for information should be addressed to:
Zonderkidz, 3900 Sparks Drive, Grand Rapids, Michigan 49546

ISBN: 978-0-310-72349-3

Published in association with the literary agency of D.C. Jacobson & Associates LLC, an Author Management Company.
www.dcjacobson.com

Zonderkidz is a trademark of Zondervan.

Editor: Barbara Herndon
Art direction and design: Kris Nelson/StoryLook Design

Printed in China

14 15 16 17 18 19 /DSC / 21 20 19 18 17 16 15 14 13 12 11 10 9 8 7 6 5 4 3 2 1

MEET THE
RANCH HANDS

Uncle Clint   Conrad   Imogene Louise   Crusty the Cook   Giddy the Wrangler

I hear that becoming a cowboy can be dangerous. Especially if you don't know the rules.

I don't know the rules.

So when I decide to spend my summer in cowboy training, the first thing I pack is my Mega Ultimate Extreme First Aid Kit.

As soon as I get to Uncle Clint's ranch, he surprises me with genuine cowboy clothes. But he forgets to tell me a teensy-weensy cowboy rule:

Do not squat with spurs on.

Right away, it is a two-bandage day.

It is also the moment I meet Imogene Louise Lathrop, the cowgirl next door. Imogene must know all about cowboy rules because she spouts, "There's more to being a cowboy than wearin' the boots."

"I know THAT," I say. "A cowboy also needs a Mega Ultimate Extreme First Aid Kit ... and a horse."

I don't think I should tell Imogene that I am missing the horse part. Uncle Clint says his horses are "too spirited for greenhorns," but he promises to buy me one at the livestock auction on Friday.

My cowboy training begins Monday morning when Giddy the Wrangler teaches me to lasso.

Somebody should have told me there is a "no lassoing pigs" cowboy rule.

Somebody besides Imogene.

"When you wallow with pigs, expect to get dirty."

"Don't worry," I tell her. "I have Mega Ultimate Extreme Cleansing Wipes."

Imogene helps me pull Snout back to the barn, where I try to pet an untamed barn cat.

"Don't mess with somethin' that ain't botherin' you none," she warns.

There are only two things "botherin'" me:

1.

Imogene Louise Lathrop.

2.

Using all of my small adhesive
bandages on cat scratches.

My second day of cowboy training, Crusty the Cook shows me his secret recipe for Chuck Wagon Chili. He even lets me add the cayenne pepper.

"A cowboy knows the difference between tablespoons and teaspoons," Imogene huffs.

I'm pretty sure Imogene made up that rule, but I wish I'd known it anyway. Especially since there is nothing in my first aid kit for hot tongues.

After dinner, the cowboys and I ride out to check on the herd.

"If you ain't makin' dust you're eatin' it!" Imogene yells.

"Don't worry!" I yell back. "I'm wearing my Mega Ultimate Extreme Protective Goggles."

When I get my horse, Imogene will be the one wearing goggles.

The third and fourth days of cowboy training, I discover a couple
of rules without Imogene's help:

Never wave a red sweatshirt at a rodeo.

Do not sneeze while pitching horseshoes.

I am applying an Instant Disposable Ice Pack when Imogene appears.

"You will always be a tenderfoot, Conrad Bates."

"Not when I'm riding my new horse," I say.

Uncle Clint and I get to the auction early. We are rubbing a Tennessee Walker's chin when a know-it-all voice says, "Admire a big horse, saddle a small one."

I choose a fine LITTLE horse named Old Nelson. We like each other right away.

While we wait to bid on Old Nelson, I invent a new cowboy rule:

Never itch your nose at an auction.

We bid and bid and bid for Old Nelson, but the price goes too high for Uncle Clint to afford him ... and the llama.

I look around to see who bought my horse.

He's mine, mine, MINE!

Crusty whispers, "Serves her right." Giddy mutters something about there being no graceful way to get down from a high horse.

I use up two disposable gloves, two instant ice packs, three antiseptic towelettes, one knuckle bandage, one elbow bandage, and six medium-sized adhesive bandages.

Imogene goes home with Old Nelson. I get a llama with an attitude.

"Maybe Imogene is right," I tell Uncle Clint. "I will never be a cowboy."

"Seems to me that bein' a cowboy is mostly about heart," Uncle Clint says. "And your heart knew one of the most important cowboy rules."

"Which rule is that?"

"Forgive your enemies. It messes up their heads."

I must have really messed up Imogene Louise Lathrop's head, because the next day, she shows up and asks if she can teach me to horseback ride.

I figure she'll be a good teacher. She knows ALL the rules.

"There's a lot more to ridin' a horse than just sittin' in the saddle and lettin' your feet hang down. There are rules about riding a horse, but the horse won't necessarily know them. And the HARDEST thing about learnin' to ride ... is the ground."

"Don't worry," I tell Imogene. "I have a Mega Ultimate Extreme First Aid Kit."

VOCABULARY POETICAL

by Giddy, Cowboy Poet

CHUCK WAGON KING

When we're workin' round-up
Crusty gits a-braggin',
Listin' all the vittles
Stored in his chuck wagon:

"I've got skunk eggs[1],
chicken legs,
hen fruit[2],
tomaters;

Firm biscuits,
smoked briskets,
sourdough,
and taters.

There are beef steaks,
spiced cakes,
corn fritters,
ground coffee;

Hard cheese,
black-eyed peas,
hearty stew,
and toffee.

I stock beef shanks,
beans and franks,
hot sauce,
dark rye;

But nothin'
could be finer than
my buttermilk pie."

So if yer on the trail
And yer belly be a-draggin',
Set yer sights fer Crusty ...
King of the Chuck Wagon.

[1]Onions
[2]Eggs

Silver spikes
Prod
Unwillin',
Renegade horses to
Skedaddle forward.

GREENHORN

There once was a greenhorn named Bryce,
Who fancied that ropin' was nice,
He lassoed a stump,
Kerplopped on his rump,
And now his lil' pardner is ice.

ODE TO CAYENNE PEPPER

Pepper, oh cayenne pepper,
Yer flavor makes me loco.
I hanker fer you on steak,
Adore you in hot cocoa.

Pepper, sweet cayenne pepper,
Yer Crusty's favorite spice.
An amigo of chili,
You brighten up white rice.

Pepper, fresh cayenne pepper,
You set my lips ablaze.
Yer spirited, I reckon,
But I'll love ya all my days.

Pepper, my cayenne pepper,
The cowhands seem concerned
That you ain't keen on me,
And one day, I'll git burned.

TEN GALLON HAT

My ten gallon hat is bigger than yers
(I'm not jest showin' off...)
It's my Sunday bathtub,
And my horse's trough.

My ten gallon hat is better than yers
(I don't mean to brag ...)
But I never need a suitcase,
Or a grocery bag.

My ten gallon hat is tougher than yers
(It's my prize bull's bed ...)
But I cannot figure why
It's too small fer my head.

TENDERFOOT

clumsy, beginner
fumblin', fearin', fallin'
pain, practice, growth, confidence
ridin', herdin', ropin'
athletic, expert

WRANGLER

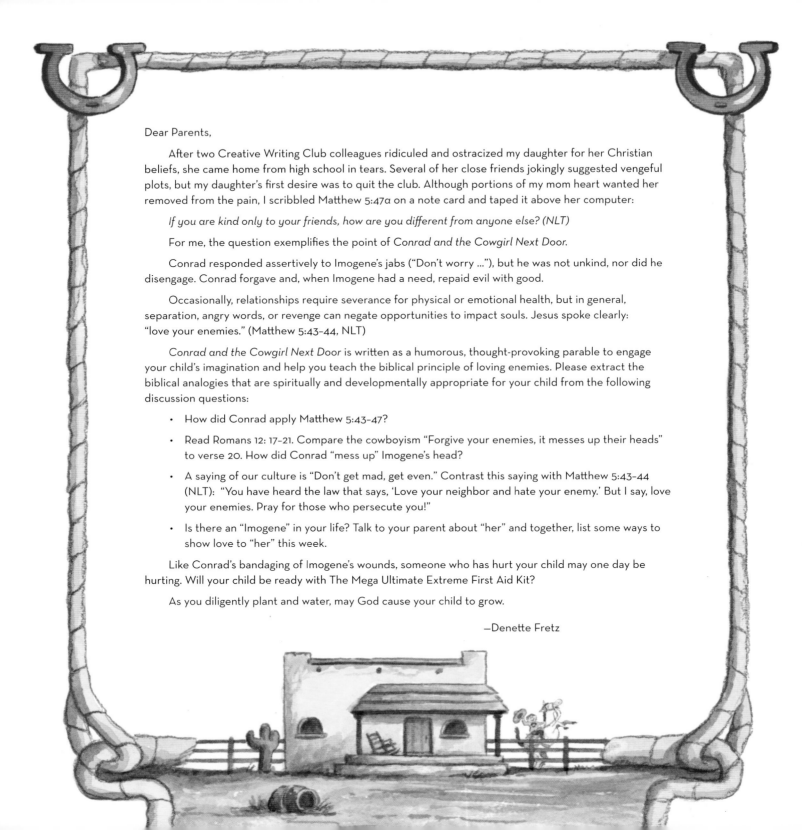

Dear Parents,

After two Creative Writing Club colleagues ridiculed and ostracized my daughter for her Christian beliefs, she came home from high school in tears. Several of her close friends jokingly suggested vengeful plots, but my daughter's first desire was to quit the club. Although portions of my mom heart wanted her removed from the pain, I scribbled Matthew 5:47a on a note card and taped it above her computer:

If you are kind only to your friends, how are you different from anyone else? (NLT)

For me, the question exemplifies the point of *Conrad and the Cowgirl Next Door.*

Conrad responded assertively to Imogene's jabs ("Don't worry ..."), but he was not unkind, nor did he disengage. Conrad forgave and, when Imogene had a need, repaid evil with good.

Occasionally, relationships require severance for physical or emotional health, but in general, separation, angry words, or revenge can negate opportunities to impact souls. Jesus spoke clearly: "love your enemies." (Matthew 5:43-44, NLT)

Conrad and the Cowgirl Next Door is written as a humorous, thought-provoking parable to engage your child's imagination and help you teach the biblical principle of loving enemies. Please extract the biblical analogies that are spiritually and developmentally appropriate for your child from the following discussion questions:

- How did Conrad apply Matthew 5:43-47?

- Read Romans 12: 17-21. Compare the cowboyism "Forgive your enemies, it messes up their heads" to verse 20. How did Conrad "mess up" Imogene's head?

- A saying of our culture is "Don't get mad, get even." Contrast this saying with Matthew 5:43-44 (NLT): "You have heard the law that says, 'Love your neighbor and hate your enemy.' But I say, love your enemies. Pray for those who persecute you!"

- Is there an "Imogene" in your life? Talk to your parent about "her" and together, list some ways to show love to "her" this week.

Like Conrad's bandaging of Imogene's wounds, someone who has hurt your child may one day be hurting. Will your child be ready with The Mega Ultimate Extreme First Aid Kit?

As you diligently plant and water, may God cause your child to grow.

—Denette Fretz